The illustrations for this book were created with black
crayon, charcoal, and gouache, with additional digital
color and styling rendered in Adobe Photoshop.

Library of Congress Cataloging-in-Publication Data

Salerno, Steven, author, illustrator.
Wild child / by Steven Salerno.
pages cm
Summary: A howling human baby causes ferocious jungle
animals to tremble until they try to tame it.
ISBN 978-1-4197-1662-1
[1. Babies—Fiction. 2. Jungle animals—Fiction.] I. Title.
PZ7.S15212Wi 2015
[E]—dc23
2014043012

Text and illustrations copyright © 2015 Steven Salerno
Book design by Pamela Notarantonio

Printed and bound in China
10 9 8 7 6 5 4 3 2 1

Abrams Books for Young Readers are available at special
discounts when purchased in quantity for premiums and
promotions as well as fundraising or educational use.
Special editions can also be created to specification.
For details, contact specialsales@abramsbooks.com
or the address below.

ABRAMS
THE ART OF BOOKS SINCE 1949
115 West 18th Street
New York, NY 10011
www.abramsbooks.com

To the wild child in us all.

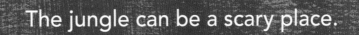

The jungle can be a scary place.

Animals **HISS**,

SCREECH,

and **ROAR**.

GNASH their teeth,

BEAT their chest,

and STOMP their feet.

They have HORNS, CLAWS, or SCALES.

In the jungle,
big and strong
always ruled.

But then a new kind of creature arrived.

It wasn't the biggest or strongest.
It didn't have sharp teeth or claws.
In fact, it was quite small, with soft skin
and only two tiny teeth.

Yet day and night all the other
animals trembled in fear of . . .

Constantly **grabbing, pinching,** and **pooping!**

Forever **pulling, kicking,** and **crying!**

Always **biting, hitting,** and **howling!**

"We must do something,"
said the Lion, his ears ringing
from being howled into.

"And soon!" added the
Rhino, her toes tender
from being bitten.

"But what?" cried the Crocodile,
his tail sore from being pulled.

"We must tame that wild thing!" declared the Hippo.

So the Giraffe tried taming the wild child
first, by feeding it leaves.
To giraffes, leaves are a tasty treat.

Next the Elephant tried taming the wild child
by spraying it with water.
Elephants love cool showers.

The Vulture tried taming the wild child
by perching it atop a tall tree.
Vultures think high places are fun.

The Anteater tried taming the wild child
by feeding it bugs.
To anteaters, bugs are like candy.

The Hippo tried taming the wild child
by rolling it in mud.
Hippos find mud to be soothing.

And the Lion tried taming the wild child
by roaring at it.
Lions like roaring at everything.

But nothing worked.

The wild child just got *wilder*.

Then the Gorilla had a clever idea.
She would try taming the wild child
by doing the *opposite* of what all
the others had tried.

So instead of
leaves and bugs,
the Gorilla fed it a sweet banana.
Suddenly, the wild child
stopped howling.

Instead of getting it muddy and wet,
the Gorilla cleaned and dried the wild child.
Suddenly, it stopped kicking.

Instead of perching it high up in a tree or roaring at it, the Gorilla cradled it in her arms while sitting quietly in the grass. Suddenly, the wild child stopped fidgeting and finally became calm.

Then it took a nap.

The animals all let out a big sigh of relief
because the wild child was now a *mild* child.

And the jungle was not such a scary place anymore.